T0132027

Mr. Joe Fish and his Fat Cat

BONNIE MICHAEL LEGACY

ILLUSTRATED BY GAIL JACALAN

iUniverse books may be ordered through booksellers or by contacting:

iUniverse
1663 Liberty Drive
Bloomington, IN 47403
www.iuniverse.com
844-349-9409

Because of the dynamic nature of the Internet, any web addresses or links contained in this book may have changed since publication and may no longer be valid. The views expressed in this work are solely those of the author and do not necessarily reflect the views of the publisher, and the publisher hereby disclaims any responsibility for them.

Any people depicted in stock imagery provided by Getty Images are models, and such images are being used for illustrative purposes only. Certain stock imagery © Getty Images.

ISBN: 978-1-6632-3939-6 (sc)
ISBN: 978-1-6632-3940-2 (e)

Library of Congress Control Number: 2022908266

Print information available on the last page.

iUniverse rev. date: 06/01/2022

I would like to dedicate this book to Parker, a girl with just one sentence, inspired me to pursue a dream. Also to my husband, Joseph for his encouragement and support.

Mr. Joe Fish loved his cats.

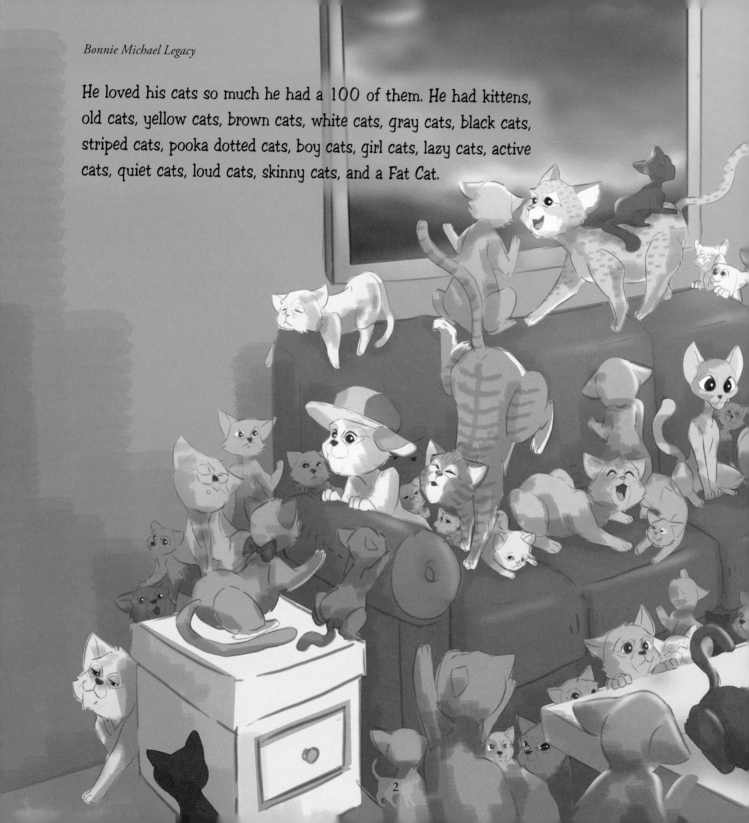

He loved his cats so much he had a 100 of them. He had kittens, old cats, yellow cats, brown cats, white cats, gray cats, black cats, striped cats, pooka dotted cats, boy cats, girl cats, lazy cats, active cats, quiet cats, loud cats, skinny cats, and a Fat Cat.

2

Mr. Joe Fish and his Fat Cat

3

Mr. Joe Fish took very good care of his cats. He would feed them, give them water, and pet them.

He would build them little houses to climb on, buy them toys to play with and hold them. Mr. Joe Fish loved his cats.

One day while taking care of his cats, he noticed one was missing. He could see his kittens, old cats, yellow cats, brown cats, white cats, gray cats, black cats, striped cats, pooka dotted cats, boy cats, girl cats, lazy cats, active cats, quiet cats, loud cats, skinny cats, but his could not find his Fat Cat.

Mr. Joe Fish looked around the food and water bowls. He could not find Fat Cat. Can you find the Fat Cat?

Mr. Joe Fish looked in the houses. He could not find Fat Cat.
Can you find the Fat Cat?

Mr. Joe Fish looked in the toy box. He could not find Fat Cat.
Can you find the Fat Cat?

Mr. Joe Fish could not find his Fat Cat. He became worried and started to search for her outside.

Mr. Joe Fish walked down the dirt road, where she liked to wander. He could not find Fat Cat. Can you find the Fat Cat?

Mr. Joe Fish went to the pond, where she liked to splash around. He could not find Fat Cat. Can you find the Fat Cat?

Mr. Joe Fish went to the park, where she liked to play. He could not find Fat Cat. Can you find the Fat Cat?

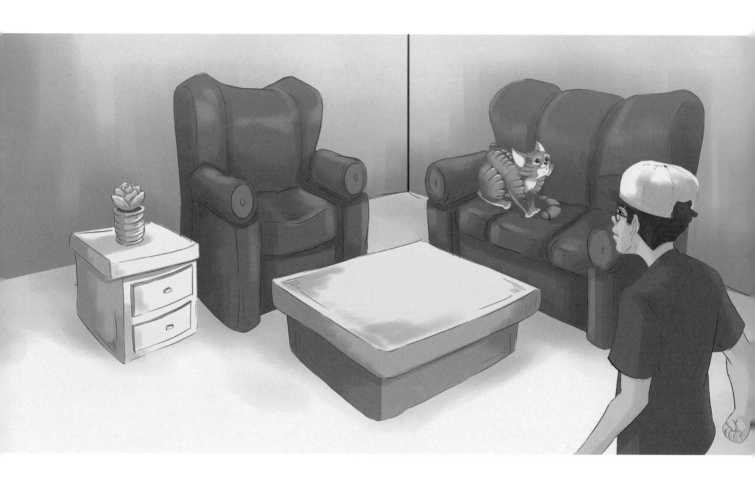

Mr. Joe Fish was so worried about his Fat Cat. He went home to look some more. When he got home, he found Fat Cat waiting for him on the couch.

For even though, the Fat Cat liked to wander and splash and play, her favorite place was with Mr. Joe Fish. Mr. Joe Fish loved his Fat Cat and his Fat Cat loved him.

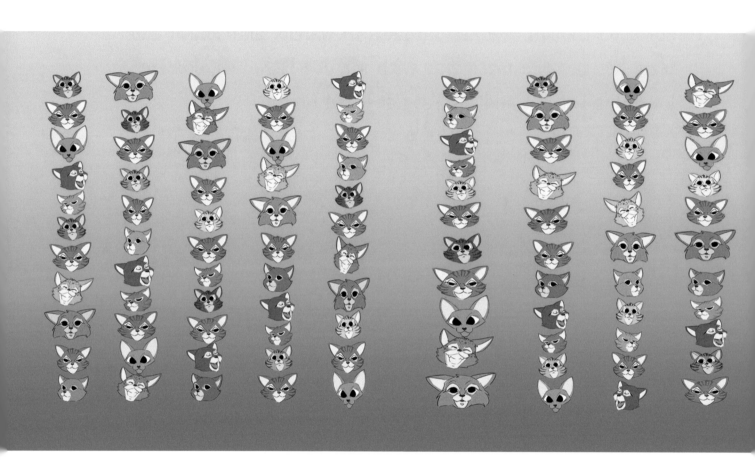

Just like Mr. Joe Fish loves his Fat Cat, so God loves you. He would leave 99 others to find you.

"What man of you, having an hundred sheep, if he lose one of them, doth leave the ninety and nine in the wilderness, and go after that which is lost, until he find it? [5] And when he hath found it, he layeth it on his shoulders, rejoicing. And when he cometh home, he calleth together his friends and neighbours, saying unto them, Rejoice with me; for I have found my sheep with was lost." Luke 15:4-6

Printed in the United States
by Baker & Taylor Publisher Services